A Home for Sally

STENETTA ANTHONY

ISBN 978-1-64003-726-7 (Paperback)
ISBN 978-1-64003-727-4 (Digital)

Covenant Books, Inc.
11661 Hwy 707
Murrells Inlet, SC 29576
www.covenantbooks.com

A Home for Sally is dedicated to every dog
who is anxiously awaiting adoption.

*M*rs. Brooks had tried to get people who were visiting her home to take one or more of her puppies without success.

After some time and with a sorrowful heart, she decided to take her puppies to the Lovin Care Kennel.

Mrs. Brooks heard this canine housing facility had a good adoption program, and that her puppies would soon be placed with a loving family.

As Mrs. Brooks entered the kennel with her puppies, they all walked in without difficulty, each one except Sally who was limping. Sally was born with a physical handicap; she did not have a front left paw.

Time at the kennel went by fast for Sally's siblings. Each of them was adopted within one month of being at the kennel. However, Sally's time at the kennel went by much slower. It had been nine months, and Sally still had not been adopted.

Waiting to be adopted was miserable for this puppy. With tears rolling down her fur, Sally would often think, "When is it my turn? "When is someone going to adopt me? I have no brothers and sisters to play with. Most of my doggie friends are gone. I'm the last one left. By the time someone adopts me, I'm will no longer be a cute little puppy, but a full-grown dog with a big deformity."

National Pet Adoption Month was soon approaching. It was the special time of the year when many people would visit the kennel, looking to adopt a canine.

To prepare for this special month, all the dogs in the kennel were groomed; their nails were clipped, polished, and their doggie fur brushed to a shiny coat.

All the dogs enjoyed this special treatment; everyone except Sally. She wouldn't let the groomers put polish on any of her nails. She felt it was too embarrassing to have only three of her nails polished.

After each dog was groomed, they were confident they would be adopted, including Sally.

Monday morning came, and Kris, the owner of Lovin Care said to all the dogs, "Okay everyone be on your best behavior. I want each of you to be adopted and have a new home."

As the doors opened people began to come in. The kennel was super busy from the time they opened until the time they closed. Excitement was in the air; children were running and playing with all the different dogs.

As the children played, some of them would point to Sally, saying, "Look at that funny looking dog. She can't even run."

This was frustrating for Sally, because she couldn't run but could only limp behind the children.

National Pet Adoption Month was almost over, and Sally still hadn't been adopted. She was feeling sadder and sadder by the day.

Watching as her friends were being adopted, Sally would walk to the mirror looking at herself. She thought about what her doggie friends Bobo and Zoomie said to her, repeating it over in her mind. "You're not worth adopting. Who wants to adopt a deformed puppy?" She walked away from the mirror with her head hanging down, holding back her tears.

Later that evening, when Kris was at Bobo, Zoomie, and Sally's cages, she patted each on them on the head. "Don't be sad, guys. You'll have a home soon."

Sally barked at her two friends and said, "Soon? When is soon? I can't go through this rejection much longer. If I'm not adopted, I don't know what I will do." Crying softly as she walked to the back of her cage.

It was the last day of National Adoption Month, and Sally was still waiting to be adopted. Only two customers had come into the kennel that day, and they were only purchasing toys for their new pets. No one was looking to adopt.

"Well," said Kris, "I think I'm going to close a little early today. We haven't had any customers for hours—"

But before she could finish her sentence, the doors opened. In walked a couple with their child.

They walked to the counter and began asking questions about the adoption process. While Kris was answering the couple's questions, their child walked around the store. He went from one end of the store to the other, never seeing Sally.

Going back to his mom, he asked, "Where are all the dogs? I thought we were coming to get me a new puppy?

Looking at her child, the mother replied, "Son, be patient, this is a big decision; I'm sure they have some dogs somewhere in the store."

"Okay, Mom," replied the boy. As he walked toward the back of the kennel, he opened the door, and there was Sally standing by her cage. For a moment, she looked up with excitement, but then turned her head.

Putting his hand out the little boy said, "Come here, doggie." Sally didn't move. Again the boy said, "Come here, doggie." Slowly, Sally limped to the boy.

As he looked into Sally's eyes, he said, "I think I've found my new puppy! This is the one!" Jumping up and down with excitement, the boy ran back to the front of the store. He said, "I found our puppy! Come look and see. This is the one I want!" Hearing this, Sally's ears perked up. "Maybe this is the day," she said!

Walking over to the cage, the parents looked at Sally and whispered to Kris, "Where's the dog's paw?" Kris began to explain that Sally was born without one of her paws, but other than that, she was a normal dog and she was the last of her litter to be adopted. She is nine months old and was the star student in her obedience class. Sally is great with children and has had all her vaccinations.

As the couple talked, Sally waited, limping back and forth in her cage. It seemed to take forever. Sally wondered, "What is the couple going to do?"

Calling to Kris, the couple said, "We've made our decision. We are going to adopt Sally."

Hearing the news from her cage, Sally began to limp around excitedly! She was finally going to be adopted.

Sally couldn't wait to have her adoption papers signed and go to her new home. As the papers were signed, Sally proudly looked at her new family with a small tear rolling down her fur, thinking, "Someone finally wanted me—deformity and all."

As the boy carried Sally out of Lovin Care Kennel, she became a little sad looking back at her friends Bobo and Zoomie sleeping in their cages. Wondering if they would ever be adopted …

Mini Dictionary

Adopt, adoption: To take up and practice as one's own, to accept formally and put into effect.

Deformity: A physical blemish or distortion.

Handicap: Having a physical or mental disability that limits activity.

Kennel: A shelter for a dog or cat.

Prospective: The act of looking forward; something that is awaited or expected.

Vaccinations: To administer an injection.

Pet Adoption Resource

1. Animal House Shelter, Inc.

   13005 Ernesti Road

   Huntley, Illinois 60142

   www.animalhouseshelter.com

2. Anti-Cruelty Society

   157 W. Grand Avenue

   Chicago, Illinois 60654

   (312) 644-8338,

   www.anticruelty.org

3. National Mill Dog Rescue

   PO Box 88468

   Colorado Springs, CO 80908

   (719) 445-6787

   www.milldogrescue.org

   customerservice@nmdr.org

4. PAWS Chicago- North Shore
   Adoption Center

   1616 Deerfield Road

   Highland Park, IL 60035

   www.pawschicago.org

   adoptions@pawschicago.org

   Puppyfind.com

About the Author

Stenetta Anthony was born and raised in the Midwest. She was a preschool educator before becoming an author. Her creative talent was enhanced and developed while educating young minds. Being in a classroom atmosphere produced her ability to write books that are educational, insightful, and thought provoking. She resides in Illinois with her husband, children, and grandchildren where loving life to the fullest is her and her family primary goal.

CPSIA information can be obtained
at www.ICGtesting.com
Printed in the USA
LVHW071356240920
666907LV00016B/535